I0692572

United States Congress

Memorial addresses on the life and character of Edward F.

McDonald, a representative from New Jersey

United States Congress

Memorial addresses on the life and character of Edward F. McDonald, a representative from New Jersey

ISBN/EAN: 9783337200916

Printed in Europe, USA, Canada, Australia, Japan

Cover: Foto ©Raphael Reischuk / pixelio.de

More available books at **www.hansebooks.com**

HON. EDWARD F. McDONALD.

MEMORIAL ADDRESSES

ON THE

LIFE AND CHARACTER

OF

EDWARD F. McDONALD,

A REPRESENTATIVE FROM NEW JERSEY,

DELIVERED IN THE

HOUSE OF REPRESENTATIVES AND IN THE SENATE,

FIFTY-SECOND CONGRESS.

PUBLISHED BY ORDER OF CONGRESS.

WASHINGTON:
GOVERNMENT PRINTING OFFICE.
1893.

Resolved by the House of Representatives (the Senate concurring), That there be printed of the eulogies delivered in Congress upon Hon. Edward F. McDonald, late a Representative from the State of New Jersey, 8,000 copies, of which 2,000 copies shall be delivered to the Senators and Representatives of the State of New Jersey, and of those remaining 2,000 copies shall be for the use of the Senate and 4,000 copies for the use of the House; and the Secretary of the Treasury be, and he is hereby, directed to have printed a portrait of said Edward F. McDonald to accompany said eulogies. That of the quota of the House the Public Printer shall set apart 50 copies, which he shall have bound in full morocco with gilt edges, the same to be delivered, when completed, to the family of the deceased.

Agreed to in the House of Representatives, February 18, 1893.

Agreed to in the Senate, February 24, 1893.

2

PROCEEDINGS IN THE HOUSE OF REPRESENTATIVES.

ANNOUNCEMENT OF DEATH.

DECEMBER 5, 1892.

Mr. ENGLISH, of New Jersey: Mr. Speaker, I rise to perform the painful duty of announcing the death of the Hon. EDWARD F. McDONALD, lately a Representative in this House from the State of New Jersey.

I shall not at the present time say anything concerning the merits of the dead, but at an early date I shall ask this House to fix a day on which his friends may express in proper terms their sense of his merit and their grief at his loss.

I offer the resolution which I send to the Clerk's desk, for which I ask immediate consideration.

The Clerk read as follows:

Resolved, That this House has heard with deep sorrow of the death of the Hon. EDWARD F. McDONALD, late a Representative from the State of New Jersey.

Resolved, That a copy of the foregoing resolution be transmitted to the family of the dead member.

Resolved, That the Clerk be directed to communicate a copy of these resolutions to the Senate.

Resolved, That as a further mark of respect for the memory of the dead this House do now adjourn.

The resolutions were agreed to.

Accordingly (at 1 o'clock and 37 minutes p. m.) the House adjourned until to-morrow at 12 o'clock noon.

3

EULOGIES.

The SPEAKER. The Clerk will read the special order.

The Clerk read as follows:

Resolved, That Saturday, the 11th of February, 1893, beginning at 3 p. m., be set apart for the purpose of paying tribute to the memory of the Hon. EDWARD F. MCDONALD, lately a Representative from the Seventh district of New Jersey.

Mr. GEISSENHAINER. I offer the resolutions which I send to the desk.

The Clerk read as follows:

Resolved, That after the conclusion of the memorial proceedings concerning the memory of the late EDWARD F. MCDONALD, now begun as the special order of the day, the House as a further mark of respect to the memory of the dead member will stand adjourned.

Resolved, That the Clerk communicate the foregoing resolution to the Senate, and that he also transmit a copy to the family of the dead.

5

ADDRESS OF MR. ENGLISH, OF NEW JERSEY.

Mr. SPEAKER: An unexpected attack of illness has so prostrated my physical powers and disordered my thoughts that I shall beg the indulgent patience of the House while I endeavor in a few words to do justice to the memory of our late fellow-member and my own old-time friend.

EDWARD FRANCIS McDONALD, recently a member of this House from the Seventh Congressional district of New Jersey, died at his residence in the town of Harrison on the 5th of November last, after a brief illness, in the forty-ninth year of his age.

Born in Ireland, he came to this country as a child, and grew up with us as one of us, and, having but faint memories of his native land, became so identified with his adopted country, was filled with the spirit of her institutions—so permeated by a love for her freedom, her Constitution, and her laws, so versed in her history and traditions, that it may be said of him without an abuse of terms that he became a typical American.

He showed his love for his adopted country by imperiling his life in the defense of the Union, at an early age. When barely 17 years old he enlisted in the war between the United States and the seceding States of the South; served with McClellan in all of the battles of the Peninsula and elsewhere with such zeal and devotion to the cause of duty that his immature constitution gave away before the fatigue and strain necessarily involved. Shattered by exposure and toil he was forced, sorely against his will, to a hospital, where under careful treatment he gradually but partially recovered and was granted an honorable discharge from the service.

Returning to his home, broken in health, he endeavored to recover bit by bit the break in his shattered constitution by falling back into the calm pursuits of private life. There he soon attracted attention as he grew towards manhood, as he acted as a man amongst those around him; and whether he lived in the city which I have the honor to represent or in the adjacent town of Harrison, to which he had at length removed, his frankness, his courage, his honesty, and his genial courtesy soon gained for him the respect and confidence and the admiration of all.

Elected to the legislature of his State, he refused further political distinction, and he set himself steadily to the task of maintaining his young and growing family. Then his career began, because his fellow-citizens, appreciating his work and its merits, struck with his manliness and worth, the direct and commanding eloquence of which he was master, called him into its political service. He was chosen at a very critical period of the country's history to the directorship of the board of chosen freeholders, and his skill soon brought order out of confusion and placed the monetary affairs of that municipality upon a firm and sound basis. Reëlected, he declined further political distinction and went back to maintain himself and his by industry and fair play, only retaining the treasurership of the town of Harrison, whose finances he had managed successfully and skillfully for a number of years.

But a man like McDONALD was not to remain long without position, and he was called again into the public service, and called in a marked manner.

There was a peculiar manliness about him, for I knew him well for years, and I speak of him as I found him. There was a manliness and directness of purpose that won him friends in the social circle, as his knowledge of public affairs and his well-balanced intellect gained him friends of a more enduring kind.

But there was one peculiarity about McDONALD which it were well that other men should imitate. When once he conceived that a course was right, when his judgment approved it, he persevered in it regardless of obstacles and careless of consequences. Thus it was that when Mr. Cleveland was nominated for the Presidency my late colleague misunderstood some of his language and so misconstrued his view. He was at that time on the electoral ticket, a compliment rarely paid to a man of his age. He promptly withdrew his name; and as he could not go over to the Republicans, with whose policy he had no sympathy, he supported a third candidate.

This of itself would have been the death blow to the political aspirations of an ordinary man within a political party; but it had no effect on the fortunes of McDONALD. His Democratic fellow-citizens, while they deplored his attitude, had such confidence in his righteousness and intent that when that episode was over they showered on him their honors.

He was elected to the State senate and to a seat in this House of Representatives, to which he would have been doubtless reëlected had not death interposed.

Of the peculiar characteristics of the man I have spoken, but feebly, because I am in that condition that it is with difficulty that I stand on my feet—the peculiar characteristics of the man were well known to me. We lived in adjacent counties, we were joined together for many years in political action, and stood together in the fight for the emancipation and self-government of a race to which we both proudly trace our descent, and there grew up between us a firm though not demonstrative friendship, and to me his loss is severe.

I remember, Mr. Speaker, as though it were but yesterday, standing at this desk, then his, now mine, a day or two after ceremonies of this kind has been performed in the House, and we had both remarked upon the unusual length of an address of eulogy, a very good one in its way, but extraordinarily long, that had been delivered. I recollect saying to him, standing just here where I now stand, in that light way with which men in health ordinarily speak of death: "MAC., in the course of nature, at my advanced age, it is possible—even probable—that I shall die before the expiration of this Congress. In that case, if you see fit to say anything about me, I hope you will not make it of an unconscionable length."

Putting his hand on my shoulder, with that bluff cordiality and caressing motion which was his way, he said: "If I have occasion to do that, I shall make it brief: but, my dear old friend, it will be strong."

Light and careless words! How little we know of the future. I have to do to-day for him that which he was to have done for me. I am here, but he is gone. I stand peering into the dim darkness beyond by the margin of that deep river which he has crossed. The old and gnarled oak that has braved the blasts of seventy-three winters still stands erect, while the stately maple in the pride of its mid age, that gave such promise of continued leafage and vigorous growth, lies prone upon the earth, felled by the ax of the woodman Death. [Applause.]

ADDRESS OF MR. GEISSENHAINER, OF NEW JERSEY.

Mr. SPEAKER: When the gavel fell upon the last hour of the first session of the Fifty-second Congress, it came, as all other earthly things, with no premonition of the future.

Happy it is that the veil is drawn upon coming events. If the storms and disappointments of life could be foreseen before entering upon the voyage, and the choice were permitted, few would have the courage to begin the journey.

Well for ourselves and for the world that the hardships and

gloom are hidden. Each one in life must do his part, and who can deny that the part, however humble and small, is not necessary to make the whole structure complete, and that it may not fill some most important gap over which an event vitally essential for the progress and well-being of his comrades is destined to pass.

The builder of the bridge may never cross upon it, and yet there may be thousands to whom the bridge will prove a means of hope and liberty and life.

It has happened that with the last finishing blow has come the ending of the one who has delivered the same.

In every phase of life are some who must prepare the way over which future generations are to successfully tread. If all were inert no path would be made, and the world remain unexplored and chaotic. So with the brother who claims our mournful remembrance this day. To him there came no prolonged warning, and only a little cloud no bigger than a man's hand indicated the unexpected storm which, coming out of a clear sky, overwhelmed him.

It was not anticipated by his colleagues that his taking off would be noted as the first that had occurred in his delegation during a long number of years; in fact, memory fails to recall the eternal departure of any previous Congressional representative of his State during his official term.

Our brother, upon the adjournment of his first Congressional session, sought his home and entered immediately upon the campaign with all the energy of his vigorous nature. By day, by night, he knew and sought no rest when the work he had undertaken demanded his attention.

Though the short term of his Congressional life had not given him full opportunity to become acquainted with his duties, yet he was thoroughly conversant with the requirements of party service. Unswervingly he yielded himself to his task and made no pause until nature called upon him to forbear. When within but a short distance of the goal which he had honestly and conscientiously striven to attain, the will of Providence decreed that he should fall by the wayside.

It is a fact beyond dispute that had his strength been lengthened to the limit of the course he would have most triumphantly grasped the palm he had so fully merited.

Three days before the end he was summoned to the congress in the spirit land.

Brother MCDONALD was a fond husband and father. For him there was no greater pleasure than when, freed from his Congressional hours, he could return to his home and the family he so dearly loved.

He was of affectionate, open-hearted temperament, and when he had determined upon his course no allurements of any nature, no pressure of any kind, could swerve him from his sense of duty.

By those who knew him he was well beloved—here in the capital city the few, at home the many. His people, paying to him the only tribute in their gift, decided that he should have no successor. In this House his vacant chair still remains vacant.

In the last gubernatorial State convention Mr. MCDONALD was the choice of all assembled to preside over its deliberations. Here his impartial rulings, his genial good nature, coupled with an earnest firmness, held in harmonious control a body rife for factional struggle.

EDWARD FRANCIS MCDONALD was born in Ireland in 1844, and emigrated to this country in 1850. In September, 1861, at the age of 17, he enlisted in Company I, Seventh Regiment New Jersey Volunteers, and served under Gens. McClellan and Hooker in the Peninsular campaign and Seven Days fight.

Stricken with typhoid fever, he returned home after fifteen-months of gallant service, and was honorably discharged on December 30, 1862. He afterward engaged in his trade of machinist and toolmaker and continued thereat until the end of 1874.

After having served in the New Jersey house of assembly he devoted himself to the business of real estate and insurance.

In 1877 he was elected director at large of the board of chosen freeholders of Hudson County and served until 1881. Mr. McDonald was elected to the State senate from Hudson County in 1889, and in 1890 received the franchises of his district for Congress and subsequently a renomination.

And so his record ends, where but for the snapping of the thread it would have just begun.

Thus his mission was completed here and Providence has proclaimed that the labors given him to perform have been fulfilled.

On many an old tombstone may be found the inscription, " Pause, traveler." We have come to-day to pause reverently at the bier of our brother and to express our sympathy for his widow, the little ones so precious to him, for the tender infant upon whom his gaze never rested, and to attest that death alone does not sever the silent tie of friendship.

ADDRESS OF MR. BERGEN, OF NEW JERSEY.

Mr. SPEAKER: It is with some misgivings I address myself to this occasion. When my colleague in Congress dies I agree that it is both my duty and my privilege to say such friendly words of his life as may occur to me, and that differences in political sentiments or aims do not detract from the obligation. I do not know that McDONALD and myself thought the same about any one public measure. He was a bitter partisan and carried his feelings in such matters to the utmost. Yet they never interfered with our personal friendly intercourse.

The most anxious of his admirers therefore need have no fear that utterances at this time which do him justice detract from his memory. I could not if I would, and would not if I could, withdraw one mite of this praise which to-day is his due. At the opposite pole it gives me pleasure to bear testimony to the belief that he acted up to his convictions always.

He was an Irish boy. Born in his island home, he came in early childhood to this country with his parents; and, linked to the destinies of this land, he early learned the privileges of her citizenship and its obligations. Ireland was his mother, but America his foster parent. He knew more by actual experience of America than Ireland. He read more of Ireland than America.

> Like him who stops in bated breath
> Suspicion e'en to guard against,

he felt that his residence and interests here might sometime throw a veil between him and his native country. He was studious, therefore, of her history, and would have her memory green. No descendant of a patriot who fought in her battle of Benburb for Irish independence and lands and home had more delight in her antiquities, her heraldry, and her religion. Her stories made his hot blood hotter. Her struggles made him pant for her release. Her past was the record of his forefathers, and her future will be that of his kinsfolk. America should hold his descendants, but America united and free meant emancipation to Ireland.

When the rebellion broke out he was a boy of seventeen. But the spirit of enterprise and desire for thrift and growth which had brought his father from their foreign home to this distant land were inherited by the son, and soon made him a soldier, and placed him in the ranks of marching forces. He joined company I of the Seventh Regiment of New Jersey Volunteers, and fought with it through its bloody conflicts—amongst others in the Peninsular campaign and the Seven Days' fight. Knowing no fear, he has a record for bravery and valor. Others fell beside him, but he moved on with the advancing column always.

Sickness and a broken constitution then take him out of the army, and he returns to the avocations of peace. He learns a trade, pursues it through its drudgery till he sees a bright sky beyond; accumulates property, comes to the front, rises, gains position, and becomes prominent. Political aspirations seize upon him, and he holds the minor offices of his locality and represents his district and county in the State assembly and State senate. Later, mastering opposition, he thwarts jealous intrigue and hate and faction, cements friendships, secures combinations, and comes to Congress the accepted Representative of a most intelligent constituency.

He is in his first term, and has served but one session in this Chamber, has been nominated for a second term, and election is three days off. He is in the height of his campaign, buoyant and hopeful, not alone for himself, but also for his party. All things seem bright before him. It is at this point we are bid to pause. The halcyon has been; the end is now. November 5, suddenly, almost without warning, he is stricken down and dies.

The mellow light of the grave is never welcome. It steals in upon us sometimes unawares and touches him who is ruddiest, most vigorous, most elastic in his step, most pressing in his business, most pressed, and in an instant all is over.

So it was with McDonald. He was only 48. He had no thought of death. He thought the future was before him and the past only an earnest of what that should be. He was not a professional man in the sense that he had studied law or medicine or divinity, but he had studied the science of politics for over twenty years, and practiced it, and was an adept in its ways and skilled in its methods. He knew how to argue it and how to use it.

The fountains from which he had drunk were Jefferson and Jackson and Calhoun and Douglas. He was a Democrat pure and simple and in sympathy with all the doings of his party and of this House, except its inaction. Results were to his mind necessary to stewardship, and they were the only evidence of Republicanism I ever saw in his nature. He was probably born a Republican, but reared a Democrat. If he made mistakes they were of the head and not of the heart. He was loyal to his adopted country and loved her. The fire of his soul enthused for her development and growth. This he showed through his whole life, but latest in his impassioned speeches on the stump. It is too much to believe, though radically differing from him, that he was not persuaded of the soundness of his statements.

I do not know that he reached the ultimate goal of his ambition; probably not. Few or none do so young and when urging on. He probably was desirous of impressing himself upon this House. Politics from his standpoint wrought revolution and exacted gain.

In its extremities he lived and hoped to live. It would give no peace to his ashes to represent otherwise. He saw hopeful changes in law and government which he thought would accrue to the advantage of his party. He was too anxious to secure them speedily, and, straining himself beyond measure, prematurely died. At least so it seems, for never before did so much of promise open up to him. Death disappointed him and his friends.

This is no time to draw lessons of religious faiths and hopes. The doctrines of the recluse, of the fanatic, and the skeptic obtain alike on this floor. The best testimony we can here bear our brother is that he was neither of these. Born in a faith, he lived it, and dying cherished that hope it assured to him.

> Time takes them home that we love, fair names and famous,
> To the soft long sleep, to the broad sweet bosom of death;
> But the flower of their souls he shall take not away to shame us,
> Nor the lips lack song forever that now lack breath.
> For with us shall the music and perfume that die not dwell,
> Though the dead to our dead bid welcome, and we farewell.

ADDRESS OF MR. CADMUS, OF NEW JERSEY.

Mr. SPEAKER: When my late beloved colleague, EDWARD F. MCDONALD, was called from this sphere of usefulness I believe that this House lost a member who, had he lived but a few years more, would have been one of its most useful and conspicuous members, as well as being one of the most distinguished that the State of New Jersey has ever sent to Congress.

Cut down in the very prime of his most vigorous manhood, and in the thick of a political fight, the result of which would have inevitably returned him to this House for another term, his death is particularly sad and pathetic.

The people of our whole State, Mr. Speaker, had been watching with interest the Congressional career of Mr. MCDONALD, for they well knew that when the opportunity presented itself he would have achieved the same distinction here that he effected in every other branch of life through which he passed.

His great ability was unquestioned by even those who were his political opponents. Everybody regarded him as a man possessed of a broad and comprehensive scope of thought. Besides, he was possessed of an eloquent tongue and those graces of manner for which Irishmen are famed. He was also a student, and every year saw great improvement in his equipment for public service.

The people of New Jersey naturally regarded such a man with pride; they felt that in this House he would be able to bring new honor to our State. Anything like mediocrity was foreign to his nature, and with his progressive spirit and remarkable force of character I venture to say that his fellow-citizens would not have been disappointed in him had it been God's will to prolong his life.

Like all men possessing true merit, Mr. McDonald was modest about his achievements. He was diffident about forcing himself into a position which he was not thoroughly satisfied that he had a right to assume. For this reason he refused all opportunities for the display of his abilities during the time that he served in Congress.

Time and again have I known members who were familiar with his gifts of mind to urge him to take part in the debates of this House, but he always declined, believing that a member beginning his first term should wait until he had first familiarized himself with the routine of the House. He knew that had he lived his reëlection was assured, and he believed that during his second term was the time for him to participate in the proceedings in a manner to which his abilities entitled him. Therefore he was content to wait.

I can not recall a more striking illustration of the possibilities of this country than that which the life of Edward F. McDonald affords. He clearly demonstrated what ability, honesty, and integrity of purpose could be accomplished by one with the most humble of origins. Born in Ireland on September 1, 1844, he came to this country when only 6 years of age, and with his parents took up a residence in Newark, N. J After attending the public schools he began to learn the trade of a mechanic, and continued at that until he was about 20 years of age. At the first call for troops he enlisted in Company I, Seventh New Jersey Volunteers.

Even at this early age he showed that he was a natural commander of men, and after a brief period of service he was made sergeant of his company. On account of ill health he was compelled for a time to quit the service on the field and go to a hospital, where he was discharged in December, 1862. He then rejoined his company and served under McClellan and Hooker in the Peninsular campaign and during the Seven Days' fight.

During this memorable struggle young MCDONALD displayed great feats of valor. He was wounded in one of the last engagements in which he took part. At the close of the war he returned to his home and continued at the trade of a machinist until the early seventies; after this he engaged in the real-estate business, which he continued up to the time of his death. In 1874 he was elected from Hudson County, N. J., as a member of the State legislature. After that he was elected director at large of the freeholders of his county and was twice reëlected. He was next elected to the State senate in November, 1889, and in 1890 was elected to represent his district in this body, and had he lived would have been reëlected in less than a week from the time of his death.

As will be observed from what I have stated, Mr. MCDONALD'S career was steadily and gradnally progressive, and his development of mind was in keeping with his advance in life. Considering that he was still a young man at the time of his death, it is natural to suppose that had he lived that none of the prizes in public life to which a foreign-born citizen is entitled would have been beyond his grasp. Mr. MCDONALD possessed that fertility of mind for which talented Irishmen are characterized, and his learning was wide-ranged. There was no company in which he might be placed that he could not make himself an attraction.

A person not knowing who Mr. McDONALD was, and who had heard him converse with persons representing various callings, might have mistaken him for a physician, a philosopher, a literary man, or one who had devoted his life to the drama or to art.

His nature was full of poetry, and his manner was particularly magnetic. He was full of the milk of human kindness, and was never so happy as when making others happy.

Such in brief, Mr. Speaker, was EDWARD F. McDONALD, and in paying my last tribute to his memory I sincerely regret that I find my words inadequate to paint him as he deserves to be portrayed.

ADDRESS OF MR. CAMPBELL, OF NEW YORK.

Mr. SPEAKER: It is a truthful saying and founded on fact, that " amidst life we are in death."

A few months ago EDWARD F. McDONALD left this city for his home in Harrison, N. J., apparently in full vigor—in perfect health. To-day he is no more. He was stricken with that dread disease, pneumonia, during the early days of the late campaign and succumbed to that grim monster, Death, but a few days before the recent election.

Born in Ireland in 1844, he came in the days of his infancy to this country with his parents and acquired a good education in our public schools.

When the nation called her sons to duty, EDWARD F. McDONALD was among the first to respond, and enlisted as a private in the Seventh New Jersey Volunteers, and as a soldier endeared himself to his officers and comrades on the battlefield and around the camp fire by his modest demeanor and his bravery.

He had held many positions of honor and trust from the people of his adopted State, and filled each and all with credit to himself, and reflected honor upon his people, who in return sent him to represent them in the Fifty-second Congress. He was a candidate for reëlection when death claimed him

As a member of this House he was energetic, painstaking, and capable, and faithfully discharged his duties.

It was my great pleasure to form his acquaintance during the Presidential campaign of 1880, which acquaintance ripened into a warm and sincere friendship lasting to the end. It is therefore, Mr. Speaker, with feelings of deep emotion that I bear witness to the many splendid traits in his character— warm, generous, impulsive, and sincere—sacrificing himself at all times for his convictions. He was brave, determined, and courageous; and stood ever ready to succor the oppressed, or right a wrong. I can see him now, with head erect, splendid physique, flashing eyes blazing with that latent fire within him, lashing with eloquent tongue those who were trying to defy the will of the people or oppress the weak.

As an extempore speaker on the platforms before the people he had few equals amongst the many distinguished speakers of his State.

Being human, he had his faults, but none can insinuate that hypocrisy could find a lodgment in his noble character. Indeed, Mr. Speaker, I can say of him without an attempt at eulogy, he was without fear and above reproach.

In conclusion allow me to say that around the hearthstone and fireside, and at the camp fires where his old comrades are wont to gather, and in political councils the name of EDWARD F. MCDONALD will stand as prominently as any of them, and the example shown by him will be used as an illustration to guide the youthful aspirants to honor and fame.

ADDRESS OF MR. NEWBERRY, OF ILLINOIS.

Mr. SPEAKER: The life and services of our deceased member, EDWARD F. McDONALD, of New Jersey, better represent the peculiar civilization of this country and better illustrate its peculiar advantages to the citizen than perhaps any event that has transpired in similar cases on this floor in many years. Here is an illustration of the fulfillment of the hopes and ambitions of a workingman born and reared among the working people, eating from the table set by honest toil, of food and raiment earned by the sweat of the brow and the fulfillment of the highest ambitions of a young, striving, and energetic American boy.

My acquaintance with Mr. McDONALD was not of long standing, but began with my services with him upon the Committee on Military Affairs, of which he was a useful member. His labors on that committee involved the exercise of great discretion and the smothering of sympathies the outgrowth of his own military service, but he demonstrated his capacity to look above and beyond the mere feelings and acted from a higher standard than that of human sympathy alone. In his efforts to do exact justice as between his Government and the man, he drew a line and occupied it that few have the capacity to maintain, and I think I may say for his associates on that committee that his decisions were never influenced by his acquaintance with the man or the circumstances surrounding the case except where even the strictest martinet might not have fully agreed with him.

During his service on that committee I had the pleasure of visiting with him the battlefield of Gettysburg in a semiofficial capacity. Although but a boy during his service in the army, it was apparent that his mind had run upon military affairs and that he had grown in understanding and comprehension of the great causes as well as the magnificent results of that contest, and during several days' close communication with him in riding and walking over that great field he honored me with his confidence and recited to me much of his early history.

As a mechanic in his early life he had developed a physique almost perfect, and it was apparent that in his leisure hours he had not failed to cultivate his brain and store up everything within his reach of the history and purpose of the Government under which he lived. His conversation was broad and comprehensive. His philosophy would have done honor to our greatest scholars, and his understanding of the needs and necessities of the common people was equal to that of any man with whom I had conversed.

Unlike many men of his class he had cultivated no animosity against what is so improperly termed in this country the aristocratic or capitalistic class. He credited many of the wrongs which have crept into society, and which he fully appreciated, as the result of a generous but misguided desire to do right, and hoped with the most sincere wish that all men, whether laborers, mechanics, scholars, statesmen, or capitalists, would find a common level for the common good in the progress and growth and establishment of a great and beneficent government on this western hemisphere.

Mr. McDonald appreciated and was proud of his own attainments, fully conscious of all he lacked. He credited our form of government with all that he had attained, and made such comparisons between the class from which he had sprung with those of a like class in the monarchial countries of Europe that would satisfy all the discontented element of that country that whatever might be their reasons for discontent here, greater opportunities were yet offered to all the citizens of this Republic than could exist under any other circumstances elsewhere.

Mr. McDONALD had a vivid recollection of his birthplace and of his early landing in America, and while never forgetting the home of his childhood, was thoroughly imbued with Americanism, crediting America with everything that was conducive to the most advanced ideas of modern progression or the development of the greatest and best manhood. His love for his adopted State of New Jersey, of his home and wife and children, and his anxiety to be with them and aid in the development of the young minds of his growing family was a beautiful characteristic of his nature.

He felt a pride in his early associations as well as his later, and made every effort to so adjust his mind and acts as to faithfully represent both.

He entered politics more as a means of his own development and for the purpose of benefiting his class than for any personal ambition. He had an easy facility of expression that must have rendered him a power for good among the class from which he sprung, and he made one of those happy links between the classes in this country that give promise of the continuance of good feeling and sympathy among all the elements that make up this great and progressive country. He had reached a goal for which he had striven. He had passed through all the grades of the civil service, acting in a highly honored capacity in the legislature of his State, his county, and his city, and had made exhibition of the possibilities which the poorest may indulge in with hope and ambition to attain. It is such men as these that give hope and life to the disheartened elements that indulge in despair over the failure of governments to properly protect the interests of humble citizens in their rights.

As has been recited by his colleagues, Mr. McDONALD was born in Ireland, from among whose people this Republic has received enough of brawn and brain to have promised like vigor and progress to all the effete nations of the earth, had they displayed the wisdom to have accepted them on an equality with their own people. He early sought our public schools and passed to the workshop and the machinist's bench, graduating thence into the heart and confidence of a great and discriminating constituency, whose opportunity to know and judge of his attainments, because of daily personal contact and association, were far beyond that of the average constituency whose representatives sit on this floor.

Mr. McDONALD's life, service, and death is not the first and will not be the last, but is another example to American youth of lowly origin and limited opportunities, teaching and demonstrating the fact that no accident of birth or station is a bar to advancement under our laws and customs, but that ability, with industry, honesty, and fair economy, has a clear road and fairly contested race to the highest goal ambition may locate.

In this instance, Mr. Speaker, this House has lost what it can illy spare—a member well informed of the needs and demands of the people—one who could give counsel to it when lacking in knowledge or slow in execution, and who had the courage and ability to check extravagant demands and guide them to wise action and intelligent conclusion.

Mr. Speaker, the Military Committee of the Fifty-second Congress has delegated me to make kindly mention of their admiration of his service and ability and their deep sorrow for his death.

ADDRESS OF MR. CUMMINGS OF NEW YORK.

Mr. SPEAKER. There is a poignant grief over the death of a father or a mother, of a sister or a brother; the plaintive wailing of a mother over the loss of her first-born is heartrending; when a near and dear friend passes away the very atmosphere seems surcharged with gloom; but of all the emotions awakened by death none is more touching than those called up by the death of a comrade. They bring the battlefield again before you. The same sulphurous canopy is above you. The hum of the bullet, the whiz of the round shot, the shriek of the shell, the clash of sabers, and the shouts of the combatants again fill your ears.

The tiresome march, the weary wading of streams, the ruddy camp fire, the bubbling coffee, and the rude fare reappear. You hear again old army songs and stories, and are lulled to sleep by the piping of frogs, the music of crickets and katydids, or by the soft patter of the rain upon your shelter tent. Again you are upon picket, musket in hand, watchful and wary, on the muddy shore of the Rappahannock or beneath the soughing pines of the Wilderness. When a comrade dies life itself seems to turn backward. You live once more in the stormy scenes of thirty years ago.

Sir, EDWARD F. McDONALD was my comrade. We were comrades in war and comrades in politics. A descendant of men who cried "Faugh a Ballagh" at Fontenoy, no braver soldier ever fixed bayonet. He was a member of a New Jersey brigade not less renowned than the Irish brigade that drove the English army from the soil of France. He was of the Army of the Potomac; he fought under the eyes of George

B. McClellan and Joe Hooker; he came from the township that gave gallant Phil Kearny to the Union. There can be no greater honor for an American citizen.

My comrade entered the ranks when less than 17. His muscles and his intellect were hardened by his experience in the army. Patriotic, fervent, brave, and energetic, he brought the experience there acquired into after life. And life with him was a continuous struggle. He had neither advantages of birth nor education. From the army of the Union he went into the greater and grander army of American mechanics. Learning the trade of a machinist, he quickly became a skilled mechanic.

Anon he entered the field of politics. It was here that his army training came into play. He heard again the music of the fife and drum in new campaigns. There were more weary rivers to cross and more escarpments to carry. There were more tiresome marches, and more batteries to silence.

How bravely my comrade came to the front his record shows. It is one of unimpeachable honor. Schooled in the ranks of the followers of Thomas Jefferson, eager, energetic, and enthusiastic, he quickly won a commission in a new brigade— that of the glorious old New Jersey Democracy. In assaulting the intrenchments of his political opponents no one was more brave and untiring; no one sustained an assault in turn more obstinately. A bitter opponent of the centralizing tendencies of the Republicans, he was an ardent State rights Democrat. A man of strong convictions, he was unyielding when asked to sacrifice them. He preferred to stem the current rather than float on it. He maintained his independence despite all personal considerations.

His Irish blood had full play, although tempered at times with American prudence. He was a born fighter—a faithful friend and an unrelenting foe. Combative in disposition and fierce in conflict, he was magnanimous and kind. His heart frequently controlled his head.

There was, however, one **tenderness in his nature** illustrative of his **true manhood**. He hated his foes, he loved his friends, but he adored his family. Enmities and friendships were neglected at their call. **His home was** his center of the universe. There, in quiet happiness, he laid aside all cares and tribulations. **Friends may** regret him, comrades may mourn him, but to his family his loss is irreparable. He was a model husband and father.

This much, Mr. Speaker, have I felt myself impelled to say about my dead comrade. **Comrades were we in the war for the** Union, and comrades **were** we upon the floor of **this** House in maintaining the reëstablished fellowship of the American people as the result of that war.

His life's fight has ended; he has crossed his last river; he has heard his last tattoo. He did his duty in this world like a true soldier. I believe that when the last grand reveille is sounded and the last great roll is called in the world above, EDWARD F. MCDONALD will be there and promptly answer to his name.

ADDRESS OF MR. COVERT, OF NEW YORK.

Mr. SPEAKER: I have been impressed, and very deeply impressed, with the **sincerity of expression** which has been so marked a feature of these memorial exercises.

No merely *pro forma* utterances have come from the floor of this Chamber to day. The words spoken have been in the nature of sincere tribute to a most sincere man. Not as mere matter of form do I desire to add my own expression of respect and regret to what has been so feelingly and so fittingly uttered by those who have preceded me.

I knew EDWARD F. MCDONALD well and intimately living; I mourn him most sincerely dead. He was a man of singular directness and distinctive force. Not his was the halting policy of the time-server, not his were the uncertain methods of the mere doctrinaire. His conclusions were reached after mature and intelligent deliberation, and in an eminent degree he had the courage of his convictions. Despite opposition and adverse criticism, he dared to give free expression to his opinions and to adhere to them and abide by them in the face of all the world.

His colleagues have spoken of his earlier career and of the substantial service faithfully rendered to the community in which he lived and to the State which he in part represented on this floor.

His record here is known to us all. Modesty has been described as the attendant handmaiden of ability. This quality of modesty restrained our late associate from public utterance on this floor during his short term of service. He was quite content that those older in position should voice here the policies he had so patiently helped to frame. Within the limits of his own district and of his own State, however, his voice was often and most effectively heard in behalf of the principles in which he believed and for the cause of which he was so sturdy a defender.

> Not by the page, word-painted,
> Shall life be banned or sainted.

Not so much by polished public utterance as by patient, conscientious performance of duty shall we determine the proper measure of praise to be accorded to the living or the dead. It is to the infinite credit of EDWARD F. MCDONALD that during the whole of his active lifetime, in whatever field of effort he was employed, every obligation was fully discharged and every duty well and faithfully performed.

Our late associate felt a commendable pride in the fact that he was a graduate from the ranks of labor. The implements of the mechanic were badges of honorable distinction to him always. He laid them aside only to seize the musket when the call came to loyal men to preserve the integrity and life of the Republic.

He had been a good workman, he was a good and gallant soldier. On the battlefield, as in the workshop, his faithfulness to duty won for him honorable advancement. In a country like ours, under the institutions of free America, a man like EDWARD F. MCDONALD was sure to forge to the front, not from any self-seeking, but because his fellow-men made imperative insistance upon his promotion.

In no other country on earth, perhaps, could conditions prevail such as those presented here. In no land save ours, perhaps, could this toiler in the workshop so rise above the conditions which surrounded him and so successfully escape the environments that hedged him in. No governmental institutions anywhere give such rich rewards to the subject; and no subjects anywhere make fuller or more loyal return.

> Go, ask your despot whether
> His armed bands could bring such hands
> And hearts as ours together.

The life of EDWARD F. MCDONALD, so sharply and so suddenly ended, teaches its own lessons.

It italicizes the fact that with us, for the achievement of the very highest objective points, it is not necessary that men shall be born to the purple. It emphasizes again the fact that a sturdy manhood, a simple honesty, a loyal devotion to principle are the qualities leading upward and onward to honorable distinction.

Mr. Speaker, the House of Representatives of the United States, pausing for a space near the closing days of its present session, honors itself in doing honor to the memory of this brave, sturdy, and sincere man—to the memory of one who was in the best and truest sense a representative man of the people.

REMARKS BY HON. JAMES BUCHANAN, OF NEW JERSEY.

Mr. SPEAKER: EDWARD F. McDONALD was a man of force. He had a vigorous youth and a sturdy manhood. An orphan lad, he landed upon our shores, carrying with him nothing of fortune but a pair of strong hands, a clear head, and a determined will. Here he found those conditions of growth, of development, of influence and power which he so sadly missed in the land of his birth. Right royally did he improve those enlarged opportunities. While the boy wrought with his hands for his daily bread he improved each moment of leisure in storing his mind with useful knowledge. However severe might be his daily task, he did not relax the discipline, by study and reflection, of his mental powers.

As he grew in physical stature and strength his mind enlarged and its faculties were trained and strengthened. He had hardly reached the strength and stature of an early manhood when the storm of civil war burst over the land. The call to arms came to him as a call to duty. In his early home he had learned to love liberty and to hate slavery. To him the Stars and Stripes symbolized a higher and a better form of civilization and of government, and he entered the army of the Union. The regiment he enlisted in had the fortune to be a component part of a brigade known widely as the "Fighting Brigade." Well did it earn its title, and among those whose bravery and courage gave it distinction none were braver or truer than Edward F. McDonald.

The war over and the grand old flag again triumphant, he turned to the less exciting but none the less honorable walks of peace. He was poor, and with his hands toiled as a mechanic for bread for himself and his family. The same force of character and determination of will pressed him to the front among his fellows. First they sent him to a seat in the lower house of the State legislature, then came other honors, and then his election as a representative from his district in the National Congress. Hardly had he entered upon his enlarged sphere of his activity and usefulness when, after but a few days' illness, that magnificent physical strength became weakness, and life went out in death. A cold, caught in active campaign work, developed with unusual rapidity into pneumonia and but a day or two before his name was again to be voted upon for a reëlection to his high trust he was borne by saddened friends to his last resting place.

As I have said, he was a man of force and power. You could not be in his presence without instinctively feeling this. As these proceedings go on my eyes light upon an item in one of his county papers which speaks of the courage and determination with which he faced an angry, tumultuous throng and quelled the riot.

I remember another incident. A State convention was being held. The spirit of faction was running high, and intense and bitter feeling pervaded the body. The chairman was weak and lost control. Mr. McDonald was urged to the front. He stepped forward, grasped the gavel, and at once the convention felt it had a master. With rapidity and precision the motions were put, the business carried through, the ticket selected, and almost ere it was aware the convention had finished its business, was adjourned, and was pressing toward the trains.

He was trusted by his friends. They knew him to be true

to them, and they stood by him. No man could accuse him of forgetting past kindnesses. No one entertained, for a moment, a doubt of his faithfulness. His loyalty was not momentary but was enduring. This subjected him at times to difficulty, but it always led to ultimate success. The people like a man whom they can depend upon. Such a man was he.

He hated shams and hypocrisy. He spoke out his thought, not always perhaps, prudently, but always fearlessly and sincerely. He did not know how to dissemble. For him to believe a thing was to proclaim it. A conviction to him was a solid and enduring truth, to be proclaimed and taught. It was not my fortune to agree always with his convictions, but it was my privilege always to admire his sincerity.

He bid fair to reach a large measure of usefulness, but at the threshold of his enlarged opportunities he was cut down. The ways of Providence are not our ways, and the wisdom of events often remains hidden from mortal view. We can not fathom the purposes of the Infinite One. We can only surrender our feeble comprehension to a fulness of faith in the declaration that "He doeth all things well," and in that faith place these memorials of our love for our fallen comrade and our esteem for his many virtues upon the records of our country's representative body.

The SPEAKER *pro tempore* (Mr. Crosby). The question is on the resolutions submitted by the gentleman from New Jersey [Mr. Geissenhainer].

The resolutions were agreed to; and under the operation thereof (at 4 o'clock and 6 minutes p. m.) the House adjourned until Monday, February 13, 1893, at 11 o'clock a. m.

PROCEEDINGS IN THE SENATE.

ANNOUNCEMENT OF DEATH.

DECEMBER 7, 1892.

Mr. McPHERSON. Mr. President, I offer the resolutions which I send to the desk.

The VICE-PRESIDENT. The resolutions will be read.

The Chief Clerk read the resolutions, as follows:

Resolved, That the Senate has heard with deep sensibility the announcement of the death of Hon. EDWARD F. McDONALD, late a Representative from the State of New Jersey.

Resolved, That the Secretary communicate this resolution to the House of Representatives.

Resolved, That as a mark of respect to the memory of the deceased the Senate do now adjourn.

Mr. McPHERSON. Mr. President, a single word. It has been a practice which has recently grown up in the Senate that such resolutions should take this course. At some future time another series of resolutions will probably reach us, when I shall endeavor to pay fitting tribute to the memory of my deceased colleague in the other House.

The VICE-PRESIDENT. The question is on agreeing to the resolutions submitted by the Senator from New Jersey.

The resolutions were agreed to unanimously; and (at 1 o'clock and 16 minutes p. m.) the Senate adjourned until to-morrow, Thursday, December 8, 1892, at 12 o'clock, meridian.

H. Mis. 101——3

EULOGIES.

FEBRUARY 15, 1893.

Mr. McPHERSON. Mr. President, with the permission of the Senator from Iowa [Mr. Allison] who has charge of the sundry civil appropriation bill now pending, I desire to invite the attention of the Senate to the consideration of resolutions from the House of Representatives in respect to the death of my late colleague, Hon. EDWARD F. McDONALD, which I ask to lay before the Senate.

The VICE-PRESIDENT. The resolutions will be read.

The Secretary read as follows:

Resolved, That the business of the House be now suspended that opportunity be given for tributes to the memory of the Hon. EDWARD F. McDONALD, late a Representative from the State of New Jersey.

Resolved, That as a further mark of respect to the memory of the deceased, and in recognition of his eminent public and private virtues, the House, at the conclusion of these memorial proceedings, shall stand adjourned.

Resolved, That the Clerk communicate these resolutions to the Senate.

Mr. McPHERSON. I send to the desk resolutions which I desire to have read and considered.

The VICE-PRESIDENT. The resolutions will be read.

The Secretary read as follows:

Resolved, That the Senate has heard with profound sorrow the announcement of the death of Hon. EDWARD F. McDONALD, late a Representative from the State of New Jersey.

Resolved, That the business of the Senate be now suspended in order that fitting tributes may be paid to his memory

Resolved, That a copy of these resolutions be transmitted by the Secretary of the Senate to the family of the deceased.

Resolved, That at the conclusion of these ceremonies the Senate stand adjourned.

34

ADDRESS OF MR. MCPHERSON, OF NEW JERSEY

Mr. PRESIDENT: So frequently has the messenger of death invaded this and the other Chamber during the present Congress that we are deeply impressed with the thought that the paths of glory lead but to the grave. Again are we asked to pause in our legislative proceedings and pay a proper tribute of respect to the memory of a deceased brother.

Soon after the convening of Congress in December last I acquainted the Senate with the death of EDWARD FRANCIS MCDONALD, Representative from the Seventh Congressional district of New Jersey, who died on November 5, 1892, at his home in Harrison, N. J., in the forty-ninth year of his age. Mr. MCDONALD was born in Ireland, September 21, 1844, and while still young came to the United States with his parents and settled in New Jersey. On arriving at the proper age he received the common-school education of that time, and while yet under 16 years of age was apprenticed to a machinist, having developed great adaptability for mechanics.

On the termination of his apprenticeship, he set up in the same business for himself, following it with various interruptions till 1875. At the outbreak of the civil war in 1861, Mr. MCDONALD, though barely 17 years of age, joined the Seventh Regiment of New Jersey Volunteers, and was amongst the first to go to the front from that State. He served with credit under McClellan and Hooker in all the battles of the Peninsula and elsewhere, until disabled by a serious illness, and was honorably discharged.

After a long time spent in restoring his shattered constitution in the hospital and at his own home, he finally recovered and resumed his business pursuits. While he was interested in the local politics of his country from the time he became a citizen, Mr. McDonald's political career may be truly said to have begun in 1874, when the electors of his district sent him to the State legislature as an assemblyman, in which capacity he served with much credit one term.

In 1877 he was selected as director at large of the board of chosen freeholders of his county, and served four years, being reëlected in 1879. During this time Mr. McDonald was also chosen by his fellow-townsmen for the position of town treasurer, which place he filled so much to the satisfaction of the people that he was elected to that office again and again, until, after ten years of continuous service therein, he declined further reëlection.

When the Presidential campaign of 1884 came on, the Democratic party (to which party he had always theretofore given his allegiance and support) called upon him to serve as one of their Presidential electors, a position rarely given to so young a man. To the surprise and regret of his party associates he promptly declined to serve in the position to which he had been nominated, believing as he did that the true interests of his State and the nation would be best conserved by the election of the late Benjamin F. Butler to the Presidency.

Independence in thought and action in respect of all matters, social or political, was one of his most prominent characteristics, and he followed the dictates of his own reason and judgment without any apparent thought of what the effect might be upon his chances for political preferment. Remaining in private life for several years, he again presented himself in 1889 as a candidate for public office, that of State senator, and was returned as elected; but on the convening of the legislature his election was contested, and for partisan reasons and purposes Mr. McDonald was unseated. However, at the meeting of the succeeding legislature this injustice was corrected, his seat was restored to him, and he retained it until he resigned to take his seat in the House of Representatives, to which he had in the mean time been elected. At the beginning of the Fifty-second Congress, and while still a member of that body and also a candidate for reëlection to the same, his death occurred. He has departed. His term had not expired, but his name no longer is heard in the roll call of the House.

The State he loved and served with signal devotion has sent here no successor to occupy the seat he so worthily filled. Such, in brief, was Mr. McDonald's political career. Starting with a township office, he rose step by step to that of Congressman. An alien, and not favored by fortune, he conquered the accidents of birth, and, scaling every barrier, rose by successive steps to the highest station within the gift of the people of his district. The confidence and trust reposed in him by his constituents is best shown by the way in which they supported his candidacy to any office to which he aspired.

Frank, open-hearted, and generous to a fault, a friend as much in adversity as in prosperity, he possessed all the noble and sturdy qualities peculiar to the race from which he was descended, combined with a rare business ability drawn from his American education and surroundings. While a Roman Catholic in his religious belief, Mr. McDonald was most liberal in his contributions to all charitable objects, irrespective of any church; besides, in an unostentatious way, being the cause of happiness to many poor families.

Possessed of magnificent health and robust in build, he could stand work that would have been death to a less powerful man. Most particularly was this apparent in his political labors. The first gun fired in the campaign found him at his post; and whether working for his own political advancement or the general party success, he was untiring in his efforts until the end of the campaign was reached.

In the late election he was a candidate for reëlection to the House of Representatives, but pneumonia carried him off almost at the very moment when success was about to crown his efforts, leaving a widow and several children to mourn the loss of a kind and loving husband and father, and regretted by a large circle of friends.

New Jersey greatly mourns the loss of her able and faithful servant in the wider field of duty to which he had been so recently called; and the Congress of the nation will have reason to feel and mourn the loss of one of its valued members who loved his country with an ardent devotion, and who sacrificed his life in the endeavor to promote the success of those principles which in his inmost heart and mind (and with all his strength) he conceived to be her true and best interests.

ADDRESS OF MR. BLODGETT, OF NEW JERSEY.

Mr. PRESIDENT: After a brief illness EDWARD F. McDON-ALD, a Representative from the Seventh Congressional district of the State of New Jersey, died at his home in Harrison, N. J., on the 5th of November, 1892. In the prime of life, just when his sterling qualities were making him conspicuous among his fellow-men, "God's finger touched him and he slept."

Mr. McDONALD was born in Ireland and came to this country when quite young. After finishing his studies in the public schools he learned the trade of a machinist, and followed that business until 1875. I first became acquainted with him about 1876, when he was following his daily avocation as a mechanic.

At that time the characteristics which were more prominently displayed in after life were visible in young McDONALD.

He was a straightforward, honest, upright man. The people of his city, recognizing the worth of the young man, elected him as a member of the State legislature. He made a record in the general assembly as a careful, conservative, and able legislator, and it was in this position that he became so well and favorably known throughout his district. On his retirement from the legislature he was called upon to perform more important duties—duties that more particularly concerned the interests of his own city.

It was at a time when marked extravagance and a reckless expenditure of public moneys characterized the government of Hudson County, and the people of that county turned to Mr. McDonald to save them from the corrupt administration of the county authorities and elected him director at large of the board of chosen freeholders of that county under a special law which invested the director with a veto power absolute in all matters pertaining to appropriations made by that board. So faithfully and well did he perform the duties of that office that he was reëlected from year to year until there no longer existed the necessity for the exercise of so great a power. He was elected in 1889 a member of the State senate from the county of Hudson. At that election the grossest frauds upon the elective franchise were perpetrated by men high in official station.

During the investigation that followed Mr. McDonald bore himself with conspicuous fairness and frankness. No taint of suspicion attached to his name. Indeed, the result of the investigation so endeared him to the people of his county that he was nominated and triumphantly elected a member of the national House of Representatives, while his term of three years in the State senate was but half completed. The same industry and ability were displayed in the short time he represented his people in Congress, and he was just entering upon a more brilliant career when he was called upon to pay the debt of nature.

In the death of Mr. MCDONALD his family lost a devoted husband and a loving father, whose presence made home supremely happy; his neighbors a kind and courteous friend, whose warm heart and cordial hand always gave them sincere welcome; his district and State an able and industrious Representative, who was true to every trust.

He has gone from the cares and trials of this life to the crowning glories of eternity, but his memory will long live in the hearts of the people he represented so faithfully and well.

Mr. President, I move the adoption of the resolutions submitted by my colleague.

The resolutions were agreed to unanimously; and (at 5 o'clock p. m.) the Senate adjourned until to-morrow, Thursday, February 16, 1893, at 11 o'clock a. m.